This book belongs to

To Jimmy and Jumper!

from Lindsey and Lola x

OXFORD
UNIVERSITY PRESS

Great Clarendon Street, Oxford OX2 6DP

Oxford University Press is a department of the University of Oxford.
It furthers the University's objective of excellence in research, scholarship,
and education by publishing worldwide in

Oxford New York

Auckland Cape Town Dar es Salaam Hong Kong Karachi
Kuala Lumpur Madrid Melbourne Mexico City Nairobi
New Delhi Shanghai Taipei Toronto

With offices in

Argentina Austria Brazil Chile Czech Republic France Greece
Guatemala Hungary Italy Japan Poland Portugal Singapore
South Korea Switzerland Thailand Turkey Ukraine Vietnam

Oxford is a registered trade mark of Oxford University Press
in the UK and in certain other countries

British Library Cataloguing in Publication Data available

ISBN-13: 978-0-19-279166-5 (Hardback)
ISBN-10: 0-19-279166-4 (Hardback)

ISBN-13: 978-0-19-279167-2 (Paperback)
ISBN-10: 0-19-279167-2 (Paperback)

10 9 8 7 6 5 4 3 2 1

Printed in Singapore

Boing...

YOU CAN DO IT, Lola!

Lindsey Gardiner

OXFORD
UNIVERSITY PRESS

People say I'm really **cute**.

First they say,
'You're so sweet, **LOLA**'.

Then they say,
'Would you like a **TREAT**, Lola?'

It can be hard
to say 'NO'

and, anyway,
it would be rude to refuse . . . wouldn't it?

So I eat lots and lots of TREATS!

Sometimes I find myself slumped
by the fridge having
A MIDNIGHT FEAST.

When I can't SQUEEZE into my kennel, Marcie smiles, 'Maybe you shouldn't have emptied the fridge last night, Lola.'

♥LoLA♥

And when I can't climb onto my **FAVOURITE** chair for a nap,

Marcie decides something **must** be done.

So we go to the park. 'For some **EXERCISE**,' says Marcie.

I spot Freckles on the seesaw and I plump myself down . . .

We're just picking the flowers off Freckles,
when suddenly
there's lots of BARKING and YAPPING.

And before you can say
JAMMY DOUGHNUTS
Bandit, Darma and Jumper
whoosh past us.

Marcie and Freckles start running, too, leaving me to catch up.

At last, I see what all the fuss is about.

A new doggy playground!

Pablo and Murray . . .

Bandit and Jumper . . .

Darma and Freckles . . .

are having BAGS of fun! I want to join in.

But it's not as much FUN as I thought.
Especially with everyone yelling at me!

'Come on, Lola!'

'OVER, Lola, not under!'

'Keep going!' Marcie shouts. But I can't . . . so I stay in the tunnel.

I just want to HIDE.

In the morning Marcie is full of beans. 'We're going to get FIT!' she says.

And ONE and TWO and THREE . . .

and **FALL** to the floor!

PHEW!

'Time for a treat,' says Marcie.
'Let's go to . . .

the MARKET!'
It's full of LOTS and

LOTS of the juiciest treats.

Who needs chocolate cake after all?

Now I can **leap** onto
my favourite chair . . .

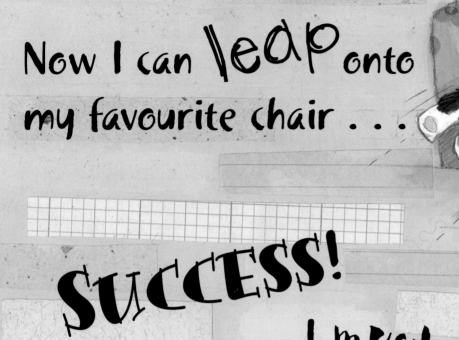

SUCCESS!

I must be getting fitter.

'COME ON, Marcie!' I say.
'We're slimmer, we're trimmer
and we're ready for the doggy playground!'

And I DO.

There are treats all round and before you can say Strawberry cheesecake,

we all **TUCK** in.